W9-AET-843

Peter and the Wolf is a musical fairy tale in which each character is played by a different instrument of the orchestra:

Peter by the violins and all
the strings of the orchestra,

the bird by the flute,

the duck by the oboe,

the cat by the clarinet,

the grandfather by the bassoon,

the wolf by the French horns,

the hunters and their gunshots by the
kettledrums and the big bass drum.

SERGEI PROKOFIEV'S

Peter and the Wolf

Illustrated by Peter Malone

Retold by Janet Schulman

Recording by the Cincinnati Pops under the direction of Erich Kunzel
Narration by Peter A. Thomas

Alfred A. Knopf New York

Early one morning, while his grandfather was still dreaming of an angel and a bear and a runaway bull, Peter tiptoed from their cottage out into the garden and past the fat duck, who blinked sleepily at him. Peter quietly opened the gate and skipped out onto the wide green meadow.

A little bird was perched on a branch of a big tree near the garden wall. He was Peter's friend. "Good morning, Peter," chirped the bird gaily. "What a fine day!"

When the duck saw that Peter had not closed the gate, she roused herself and began waddling out of the garden and into the meadow. "How nice to start the day with a swim in my very own pond," she thought.

The little bird and the duck were friends, but sometimes they liked to tease each other. Today the bird flew down onto the grass and said to the duck, "What kind of bird are you if you can't fly?"

The duck quacked back, "What kind of bird are you if you can't swim?" And she splashed noisily into the pond.

The two argued back and forth, the duck splashing and swimming in the pond, the bird fluttering and hopping along the pond's edge.

"You can't fly!" twittered the bird.

"You can't swim!" quacked the duck.

Suddenly Peter, who was watching the duck and the bird argue, saw his cat sneaking through the tall grass.

"Oh, how I love little birds," thought the cat. "And this one is so busy arguing, I'll just grab him and start my day with a lovely breakfast."

"Look out!" shouted Peter. The bird instantly flew off to the big tree by the garden wall while the duck quacked angrily at the cat from the middle of the pond.

Meanwhile, Peter's grandfather was up and about and wondering where Peter was. He came stomping through the garden gate and out to the meadow. "How many times must I tell you not to go into the meadow alone?" he scolded. "And always close the gate. What would you do if a wolf came out of the forest?"

Peter said, "I'm not afraid of a wolf."

"Silly boy, a wolf is dangerous," said Grandfather as he led Peter back to the garden, locked the gate, and went into his cottage.

And then danger came. Out of the trees across the meadow, a big, hungry wolf crept through the tall grass.

The cat was the first to spot it. In a flash, she ran to the tree by the garden wall and shot up it, climbing higher and higher until she could go no farther.

The duck still did not see the wolf. She was only concerned for her friend. "Look out for the cat, little bird!" quacked the duck as she splashed out of the pond and followed the cat to the big tree.

The poor duck did not see the wolf until it was too late. Then she waddled off as fast as she could and flapped her wings madly, trying to fly. But the wolf ran fast and faster. He came closer . . . and closer . . . and was almost upon her when he pounced—and with one big gulp, he swallowed the duck whole!

The wolf licked his lips and trotted over to the tree. He paced around and around it, staring up at the cat.

"Now he's after you," trilled the little bird to the cat.

The cat looked up at the bird and hissed, "And I'm after you."

"But you'll never catch me!" the bird chirped back.

"Come down and play with me," said the wolf to the cat, pretending to be friendly. "I won't hurt you."

Peter was watching all that was going on from behind the safety
of the closed gate. "I'm not afraid of the wolf," he said, and ran
into the cottage. Quickly he returned with a strong rope and
climbed the garden wall near one of the big branches of the
tree. He grabbed the branch, swung himself into the tree, and
whispered to the bird, "Fly down and circle around the wolf's
head, but be careful—don't get too close!"

The little bird swooped down near the wolf, and as the wolf threw his head back and snapped his jaws open, the little bird darted off.

"How dare you tease me," snarled the wolf, and he snapped angrily at the bird from this side and that. The bird would brush the wolf's nose with his wings, and just as the wolf thought he had caught the bird, off went the bird, chirping shrilly. Again and again the little bird fooled the wolf.

Up in the tree Peter wasted no time tying the rope to the big branch and making a noose with the other end. He waited until the wolf was all tired out from jumping at the bird. When the wolf stood still for a moment, Peter lowered the noose over the wolf's tail and pulled with all his might on the rope. He caught the wolf!

The wolf pulled and tugged and tugged and pulled on the rope. But Peter had tied the rope securely to the big branch and the wolf could not get free. Finally, the beast fell down in a heap, exhausted and defeated.

"Please let me go to my home in the deep, dark woods," panted the wolf, "and I will never come here again."

Just then two hunters came crashing out of the forest, looking about
nervously. They were afraid of the wolf, and when they saw it, they
began shooting wildly into the air.

"Stop shooting!" shouted Peter. "We have already caught the wolf."

The hunters breathed a sigh of relief. When they heard that the wolf
had promised never to come back, they offered to help Peter lead him
back to his home . . . so long as he was safely tied to a rope.

"Follow me," chirped the bird.

Then all of them set off for the forest.

First came Peter.

After him marched the cowardly hunters with the big, tired wolf on a rope. Then came Grandfather. "Have you ever seen a boy as brave as Peter?" he called to the hunters. "And so clever!"

And last came the cat, thinking, "Tomorrow I'll get that bird."

Over their heads fluttered the little bird, chirping happily, "Peter and I caught the wolf!"

And the duck? The duck was making such a quacking and thrashing about in the wolf's stomach that the wolf felt guilty and finally coughed her out, whereupon she joined the procession, quacking triumphantly.

THIS IS A BORZOI BOOK PUBLISHED BY ALFRED A. KNOPF
Text copyright © 2004 by Random House, Inc.
Illustrations copyright © 2004 by Peter Malone
Story and music by Sergei Prokofiev
Copyright © 1937 (renewed) by G. Schirmer, Inc. (ASCAP), publisher and copyright owner. International
copyright secured. All rights reserved. Reprinted by permission.
Orchestral recording under license from Vox Music Group, a division of SPJ Music Ltd.
All rights reserved under International and Pan-American Copyright Conventions. Published in the United States by
Alfred A. Knopf, an imprint of Random House Children's Books, a division of Random House, Inc., New York,
and simultaneously in Canada by Random House of Canada Limited, Toronto.
Distributed by Random House, Inc., New York.
www.randomhouse.com/kids
KNOPF, BORZOI BOOKS, and the colophon are registered trademarks of Random House, Inc.

Library of Congress Cataloging-in-Publication Data
Schulman, Janet.
Peter and the wolf : with the music by Sergei Prokofiev / retold by
Janet Schulman ; illustrated by Peter Malone.
p.   cm.
SUMMARY: Despite Grandfather's warning about wolves in the forest, Peter and his animal friends capture one.
ISBN 0-375-82430-8 (trade) — ISBN 0-375-92430-2 (lib. bdg.)
[1. Wolves—Fiction. 2. Birds—Fiction. 3. Cats—Fiction. 4. Grandfathers—Fiction.] I. Malone, Peter, ill.
II. Prokofiev, Sergey, 1891–1953. Petëïa i volk. III. Title.
PZ7.S3866Pe 2004
[E]—dc22
2003010516
MANUFACTURED IN CHINA
September 2004
10 9 8 7 6 5 4 3 2 1
First Edition

Peter and the Wolf is a musical fairy tale in which each character is played by a different instrument of the orchestra:

Peter by the violins and all the strings of the orchestra,

the bird by the flute,

the duck by the oboe,

the cat by the clarinet,

the grandfather by the bassoon,

the wolf by the French horns,

the hunters and their gunshots by the kettledrums and the big bass drum.